COND

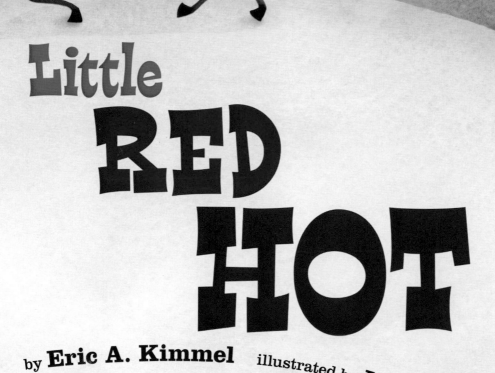

Little
RED
HOT

by **Eric A. Kimmel**   illustrated by **Laura Huliska-Beith**

Amazon Children's Publishing

A NOTE FROM THE AUTHOR

After completing **Jack and the Giant Barbecue**, I wanted to write another Texas story. How about taking Little Red Riding Hood and throwing in some hot chili peppers?

There are more than two hundred varieties of chili peppers. The hottest, at least for now, is the Trinidad Moruga Scorpion. The Scoville Hotness Scale is used to measure the heat of chili peppers. The Habanero pepper—the hottest pepper you'll find in a grocery store—has an SHU rating of 350,000. The Trinidad Moruga Scorpion's SHU rating is 2,000,000. OUCH!

Capsaicin is the chemical compound in chili peppers that causes the burning sensation. All chili peppers, even mild ones, should be handled with care. Cover your hands with plastic gloves. Use chopsticks or tongs to hold the chilies in place while preparing them. Never touch your mouth, nostrils, or eyes while preparing chili peppers.

Keep some milk, yogurt, or ice cream nearby when eating hot food prepared with chilies. Dairy products reduce capsaicin's burning sensation.

Some people love to eat hot chili peppers. Chili eating contests take place all over the world—even though contestants sometimes end up in the hospital.

To Margery —E.A.K.

**For Anna, Claire, and Ivy;
the cutest little hot peppers on the planet. —L.H-B.**

Text copyright © 2013 by Eric A. Kimmel
Illustrations copyright © 2013 by Laura Huliska-Beith

Amazon Publishing
Attn: Amazon Children's Publishing
P.O. Box 400818
Las Vegas, NV 89140
www.amazon.com/amazonchildrenspublishing
Library of Congress Cataloging-in-Publication Data
available upon request.
ISBN 9781477816387 (hardcover)   9781477866382 (ebook)

The illustrations are rendered in gouache, acrylic, and
colored pencil paintings combined and collaged on the computer.

Book design by Vera Soki
Editor: Margery Cuyler

Printed in China (R)
First edition
10 9 8 7 6 5 4 3 2 1

Once upon a time
there was a little biddy Texas gal
called Little Red Hot.

Folks called her that because she loved to eat red hot chili peppers.

She ate peppers for breakfast, lunch, and dinner.

She ate pepper ice cream for dessert.

She had hot pepper cake for her birthday with jalapeños on top instead of candles.

Folks used to say that Little Red Hot
could eat fire out of a stove.

Little Red Hot would answer, "No, I
wouldn't do that. Fire ain't hot enough."

One day Little Red Hot's momma said to her, "Little Red Hot, I heard from Grandma today. She's feeling poorly. I think she has a cold. Could you drop by and look in on her? She'd feel so much better to see you."

"I'll do that, Momma," Little Red Hot said. "I'll bake a hot pepper pie, Grandma's favorite. It'll knock those cold germs right out of her."

Little Red Hot got busy in the kitchen. In no time at all she had mixed up a hot pepper pie. She used Louisiana Hot Sauce instead of milk and filled the crust with eggs, cheese, and the hottest chili peppers she could find.

Jalapeño peppers that could make a grown man weep.

Tabasco peppers that could knock over a longhorn.

Habanero peppers that could take the paint off a wall.

And Naga Jolokias from India, one of the hottest peppers in the world. WARNING

Each one came with a warning label.
Little Red Hot put the pie in the oven to bake. She didn't have to turn the oven on. That pie was so hot, it baked itself.

Little Red Hot got on her pony and set off for Grandma's house.

Along the way she met up with Pecos Bill and his cowboys.

"Hey, Little Red Hot! Where ya goin'?" they called to her.

"I'm taking a hot pepper pie to Grandma. She has a cold," Little Red Hot said.

"Now you be careful on your way to Grandma's house," said Pecos Bill. "We just talked to Three Little Tamales. They say that Señor Lobo, the Big Bad Wolf, is prowling around the neighborhood. You keep an eye out for him."

"I'll do that, Pecos Bill,"
Little Red Hot promised.

No sooner had Pecos Bill and the cowboys ridden out of sight when Little Red Hot saw a big gray animal loping toward her.

"Hold it right there! Don't you come any closer!" Little Red Hot yelled. "I know who you are. You're Señor Lobo. Pecos Bill warned me about you."

The big gray animal stopped running.
"You got me all wrong, Miss," he said.
"I'm not Señor Lobo. I'm Señor Coyote. I
may be tricky, but I wouldn't hurt a fly."

"You're mighty big for a coyote,"
Little Red Hot said.

"You're a mighty smart little girl.
And pretty, too. Where are you going?"

"I'm going to visit my grandma. She's
feeling poorly," said Little Red Hot.

"What a good little girl you are!
You tell your grandma I hope she feels
better." And off he went.

Of course, that big gray animal wasn't Señor Coyote at all. It was Señor Lobo—and Little Red Hot had no business talking to him.

But it was too late to do anything about that now.
Even worse, Señor Lobo knew a shortcut that took
him straight to Grandma's house.
He stepped up to the front door and knocked.

"Little Red Hot, is that you?" Grandma said.
Señor Lobo made his voice sound like Little
Red Hot's. "Yes, Granny. I heard you were sick.
I hope you're feeling better."

"I feel better already now that you're here.
Come on in!"

Señor Lobo did just that.
Grandma let out a yelp when she saw
him. Grandma was sick, but she wasn't slow.

She jumped out the window and ran.

"I'll catch her later," Señor Lobo said. He rummaged through Grandma's clothes until he found a spare nightcap and nightgown.

He put them on and hopped into bed just as Little Red Hot arrived.

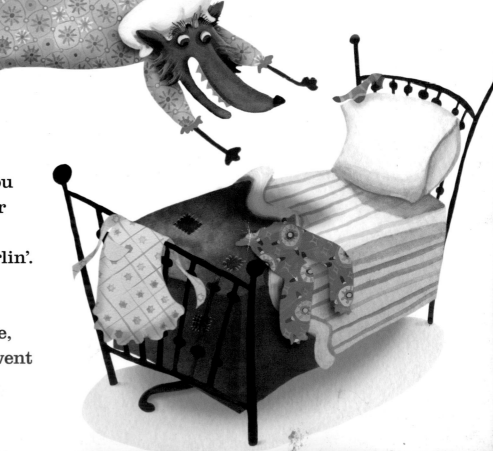

"Howdy, Grandma! It's Little Red Hot. I'm sorry you don't feel good. Why is your front door open?"

"To let in the breeze, Darlin'. To let in the breeze," Señor Lobo said.

"I brought you a surprise, Grandma." Little Red Hot went into the kitchen.

She cut a big wedge of hot pepper pie
and put it on a plate. She carried it to
Grandma's bedroom.

Señor Lobo lay on the bed with the covers pulled up to his nose. Little Red Hot looked at him real hard.

"Grandma, what **big eyes** you got!"

"The better to see you with, Darlin'," Señor Lobo said.

"Grandma, what **big ears** you got!"
"The better to hear you with, Darlin'," Señor
Lobo said.

"Grandma, what **big teeth** you got! Now don't say another word, 'cause I know what they're for," said Little Red Hot.

"What're they for, Darlin'?" Señor Lobo asked.

"They're for eatin' this
hot pepper pie
I made just for you!" Little Red Hot
shoved that wedge of pie into Señor
Lobo's mouth.

To say he yelled wouldn't do him justice. He hollered so loud space aliens could have heard him over in the next galaxy. He didn't go out the front or the back. He shot straight up like a rocket, right through the ceiling of Grandma's bedroom, trailing fire and smoke as he went.

That's when Pecos Bill and the cowboys arrived. "Grandma told us Señor Lobo came by. Where is he?"

Little Red Hot pointed up at the hole in the ceiling. "He went thataway. I don't suppose he'll be back. Would y'all like to stay for supper? I got hot pepper pie for everyone."

"No, thanks, Little Red Hot," Pecos Bill and the cowboys said. "We're brave, all right. But not that brave."

So Little Red Hot
and her grandma ate
that hot pepper pie
all by themselves.
Every last crumb.
And guess what? It
knocked those cold
germs flat out.

Just as Little Red Hot
had promised.